First published in 1996 by Sapling,
an imprint of Boxtree Ltd, Broadwall House,
21 Broadwall, London SE1 9PL
Copyright © Geoffrey Planer, 1996

10 9 8 7 6 5 4 3 2 1

Reproduction by SX Composing DTP
Printed and bound in Great Britain by Cambus Litho Ltd.

ISBN: 0 7522 2330 5

A CIP catalogue entry for this book
is available from the British Library.

MOUSE TALES

Teatime o'Clock

Geoffrey Planer

sapling

For Cassie and Ruth
and Maddie

'Is that the time?' exclaimed Mr Tail,
looking at his watch. He hung his
coat on the peg by the door.
'My word, it's half past bedtime already!'
he said as he grabbed the nearest mouse,
popped it onto his lap and sat down
in the Favourite Chair.
'How does your watch know it's
bedtime?' Tom asked.
'That's what watches are for; they
tell you what time it is. These little arms
move round and point to the numbers.'
'Do all watches tell the same time?'
asked Tom.
'They do indeed,' said Mr Tail.
'How did they know what time it was
when they made the first watch?' asked Tom.
'Herumph. I think it's time for a story,' said
Mr Tail, coughing lightly into his paw.

Another Night,
Another Mouse,
Another Tale . . .

Teatime o'Clock

A very, very, very long time ago watches weren't invented. There were no watches and no clocks; there was nothing to tell the time with.

No one minded
much, though;
they just went
on as normal,
doing their
usual things
at what they
thought was
the usual time.

Quite a long time ago, in the land of
King Eggo, there lived, in a shed,
an inventor called Coggo.

He was very clever at making new things;

even if they didn't always
work right first time.

Should King Eggo want
a thingy that would
cut paper, Coggo
tied two knives
together to
make scissors.

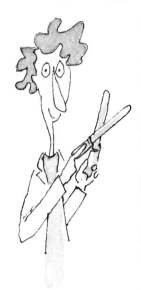

When the Queen
couldn't read some
tiny words, he glued
two magnifying
glasses together to
make spectacles.

When Mrs Baggo needed to get down
to the shops in a hurry, he nailed
two wheels to a post

(of course the wheels wouldn't go round,
so Coggo didn't quite invent the bicycle
that time; but he was pretty clever).

Now King Eggo loved eating. And his favourite meal was tea. Teatime never came soon enough. In the afternoons he and the Queen would sit at the table together.

'I think it's teatime now,'
the King would say.
'Not quite yet, my dear,'
the Queen would say; firmly.
'I think it is, dear,' the King
would answer.

'Not yet, dear.'
'My tummy's rumbling, dear.'
'Tell it that it's too early, dear.'
said the Queen.

And she carried on reading.

The King went to Coggo.

'I need something that tells me
when it's teatime, Coggo, old bean ...'
he said, '... and something that tells
it to me often; and soon; and early.'

Coggo scratched his head, and got
out his bag of bits and pieces and
started to experiment.

Next day he went to show the King
the special new box he had made.

'With this key you wind up a spring,
Your Kingship, which then unwinds very
slowly and turns this pointer on the front
of the box round, very slowly,' he said.

'And ...' he continued '... on the box we could write some numbers, or some words, so we would know what time it was.'
'Like teatime?' said the King hopefully.

'Exactly,' said Coggo, and he wrote the word 'Teatime' at the top of the box.

Excitedly the King wound the spring up
and took it to the Queen who was
sitting in the parlour, not eating
bread and honey.

He told her all about it and
put the box down on the table.

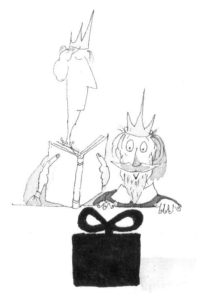

They sat and watched the pointer move
round very slowly. They watched the
pointer turn slowly towards the word
'Teatime' written at the top of the box.

The pointer moved very slowly.
Very, very slowly.
Very, very, very slowly.
It grew dark. Everyone else went to bed.

The King waited and watched alone.
At last it pointed to the word 'Teatime' on
the top. But by then the King had fallen
sound asleep in front of his new box.

The next day the King took the box back to Coggo. 'This is no jolly good Coggokins. I can't eat tea in the middle of the night,' he said.

Coggo thought hard.

'I'll just push the pointer round a bit with my finger,' he said. 'What time do you think it is now, Your Majesticness?'

'Teatime?' suggested the King.

Coggo moved the pointer so it pointed to
the word 'Teatime' at the top of the box.

'Teatime it is, Your Worship.'
'Hurrah!' said the King and
went off to have tea.

And from that day on he had his tea
at the same time every day ...

... lunchtime!

'And now it's three quarters past bedtime
o'clock ... so off you go,' said Mr Tail.
'Can I see your watch?' asked Tom.
'Certainly,' said Mr Tail, and he held
it up for Tom to see.
'Just as I thought,' said Tom.
'What did you think?' asked Mr Tail, puzzled.
'It doesn't say three-quarters-past-bedtime
at all. It says ten-minutes-to-play-time!'
And, quick as lightning, Tom jumped
from Mr Tail's lap and made a run for it.
Too bad – his run took him straight into
Mrs Tail's arms and without further ado
she marched him, and the 364 other
little Tails, straight off to bed.

*Small Tales,
Tall Tales,
Bedtime -
for All Tails*